For Maisie and Lottie Farber-Evans,
with love, Auntie Hoohee xxx ~ SM

For Sjoerd and Jenna x ~ NO

Bloomsbury Publishing, London, New Delhi, New York and Sydney

First published in Great Britain in 2013 by Bloomsbury Publishing Plc
50 Bedford Square, London, WC1B 3DP

Text copyright © Suzi Moore 2013
Illustrations copyright © Nicola O'Byrne 2013
The moral rights of the author and illustrator have been asserted

A CIP catalogue record for this book is available from the British Library

ISBN 978 1 4088 3693 4 (HB)
ISBN 978 1 4088 3694 1 (PB)
ISBN 978 1 4088 3947 8 (eBook)

1 3 5 7 9 10 8 6 4 2

Printed in China by C&C Offset Printing Co Ltd, Shenzhen, Guangdong

www.bloomsbury.com

Two Little Bears

Suzi Moore   Nicola O'Byrne

BLOOMSBURY

LONDON NEW DELHI NEW YORK SYDNEY

Here is the place where the wild river flows,
where the mountains are high,
where the wind blows, blows, blows.

High on a hill, far away from all men,
the brown bears sleep in the warmth
of their den.

All except one . . .

Quietly one bear wakes up and he creeps.
He creeps through the den where Mama bear sleeps.

He wrinkles his nose...

...and stretches a paw.

Then, with a deep breath,
he goes out to explore.

"It's not time yet," says Mama Brown Bear.
"Go back to sleep, my Little Brown Bear."

So Little Brown Bear creeps back inside.
And all is still on the mountainside.

Here is the place where the north wind blows,
where the ice fills the sea,
where it snows, snows, snows.

Cuddled up tight, far away from all men,
the snow bears sleep in the warmth of their den.

All except one . . .

The smallest snow bear wakes up and she creeps.
She creeps through the den where Mama bear sleeps.

She wrinkles her nose . . .

. . . and stretches a paw.

Then, with a deep breath,
she goes out to explore.

"It's not time yet," says Mama Snow Bear.
"Come back to me, my Little Snow Bear."

So Little Snow Bear cuddles up tight.
And dreams her way through the long winter night.

Here is the place where all things grow,
where the warmth of the sun melts the hardest of snow.

The brown bears wake and step outside.
They make their way down from the mountainside.

Little Brown Bear runs
through long wavy grass,

to the edge of the water,
where the river runs fast.

Mama Brown Bear says, "Watch what I do."
So the little bear watches, and then he does it too.

Here is the place where the time has come,
for baby snow bears to follow their mum.

They follow her out from their cosy den,
and make their way down to the sea once again.

Mama Snow Bear says, "Watch what I do."
So the smallest bear watches, and then she does it too.

Here is the place where BOTH bears come,
where the sea meets the river in the light of the sun.

On one side a brown bear – what can he see?

On the other, a snow bear – what can it be?

A brown tuft of fur,
a little white paw.

A white tuft of fur,
a little brown paw.

Then BOTH little bears set off to explore.

One little bear counting.
One little bear hiding.

One little bear running.
Two little bears smiling.

Two little bears down by the shore.
Two little bears, eight little paws.

Two little bears have much more fun.
Two little bears are better than one.

Here is the place where the wild river flows,
where the mountains are high,
and where it snows, snows, snows.

Cuddled up close, far away from all men,
two bears sleep in the warmth of a den.

Snuggled together, beneath stars so bright,
they happily dream through the cold winter night.